Greg has had it with his parents fighting. He's had enough of being blamed and criticized for everything.

Greg wants a new life. Preferably one without his father.

And the bubbles in Grenoble promise just that.

AUTHOR OF *FIRST IMPRESSIONS*

R. W. WALLACE

UNEXPECTED CONSEQUENCES

An Urban Fantasy Short Story

Unexpected Consequences
by R.W. Wallace

Copyright © 2019 by R.W. Wallace

Copy editing by Jinxie Gervasio
Cover by the author
Cover Illustration 20516303 © Alexander Sorokopud | 123rf.com
Cover Illustration 40633245 © Michal Bednarek | 123rf.com

All characters and events in this book, other than those clearly in the public domain, are fictitious and any resemblance to real persons, living or dead, is purely coincidental.

All rights reserved. No part of this publication may be reproduced, distributed, or transmitted in any form or by any means, including photocopying, recording, or other electronic or mechanical methods, without the prior written permission of the publisher, except in the case of brief quotations embodied in critical reviews and certain other noncommercial uses permitted by copyright law. For permission requests, write to the publisher, addressed "Attention: Permissions Coordinator," at the address below.

www.rwwallace.com

ISBN: [979-10-95707-35-6]

Main category—Fiction
Other category—Fantasy

First Edition

Also by R.W. Wallace

Mystery

The Tolosa Mystery Series
The Red Brick Haze (free)
The Red Brick Cellars
The Red Brick Basilica

Ghost Detective Shorts (coming soon)
Just Desserts
Lost Friends
Family Bonds
Till Death
Common Ground

Short Stories
Hidden Horrors
Cold Blue Eternity
Critters
Gertrude and the Trojan Horse
First Impressions
Let Them Eat Cake
Out of Sight
Two's Company

Adventure (short stories)
Size Matters

Fantasy (short stories)
Morbier Impossible
A Second Chance

Science Fiction (Short Stories)
Quarantine

UNEXPECTED CONSEQUENCES

The city of Grenoble slumbered under a blanket of mist. High up, above the mountainous Alps surrounding the city, the sky still appeared to be blue. Maybe. It was a bit like lying in bed at night waiting for your parents to stop fighting; you knew they'd tire eventually, and that morning would come and everyone would be okay, but in the present moment it was hard to believe.

Greg had never felt such oppressive heat before. His lungs protested the arrival of the moist air and did their best to get it back out as soon as possible. His body was covered in a sheen of sweat and his entire back was soaked through because of his backpack. He was pretty sure drops of sweat dripped to the ground behind him.

How did the citizens of Grenoble live in this climate, day in and day out? As Greg trudged down the sidewalk of the endless Cours Jean Jaures, he studied the people around him.

For the most part, they seemed to ignore the fact that they were melting away, a drop of sweat at the time. The women wore summer dresses, some skimpy, some more adapted for office wear. The men sported t-shirts or short-sleeved button-downs, mostly in fabrics that didn't darken too much when soaked in sweat.

Almost everybody glanced regularly at the sky, and many turned their heads in direction of the city center as if to check for something.

Greg didn't see anything other than large, dark stone buildings lining the avenue he'd chosen, and a blurry, small mountaintop emerging straight ahead—probably the Bastille, his reason for coming here in the first place.

He'd been walking for three days straight. He'd left Lyon Saturday night, and now here he was in Grenoble, a hundred kilometers later, with aching legs, blisters on his feet, and a sunburned nose.

But he was free, and he'd never felt better.

Still, a pause wouldn't be a bad idea.

Greg pulled his worn wallet out of his back pocket—damp with sweat, how nice—to check on his finances. He'd brought all his savings, which amounted to about one hundred and fifty euros, plus two twenties he'd lifted from his dad's jacket on his way out the door.

Just thinking about it gave him the hives, but he told himself—like he had hundreds of times since leaving home—that he'd never have to worry about his dad again. If he got mad, it wasn't Greg's problem.

It might become his mom's problem, but hey, she knew how to stand up for herself.

He had eighty euros left. Not much to live on, but he wasn't supposed to need to live here for more than a day or two more.

He could certainly afford something to drink, especially since he was feeling a little light-headed and wasn't certain he'd make it to the Bastille without some sustenance.

Spotting several red parasols and grey, metallic chairs, Greg advanced down one of the narrow, cobbled streets running perpendicular to the wide Cours Jean Jaures. The café was named *le voyageur tranquille*, which Greg found to be fitting. At least that was the goal.

He ordered a *diabolo menthe*, lemonade with mint syrup, and a ham sandwich. He eased into one of the chairs so he'd be facing the small square with its cutesy fountain and let out a contented sigh. Unable to resist, he lifted his feet to the chair opposite.

"Long day, huh?" The female voice came from Greg's left.

A girl, probably about Greg's age, with long, curly brown hair, large brown eyes, and cheeks so chubby they made Greg think of a hamster, sat at the next table with a milkshake in front of her.

"Uh huh," Greg replied and turned away from her.

"Except it's only nine in the morning," she continued, clearly oblivious to the fact that Greg just wanted to be left alone. "How'd you manage to get so tired already? Do you not practice enough sports? It's really important, you know, to stay in shape. Even at fifteen."

Greg snapped his gaze back to the girl. How did she know his age?

"You look like you're in shape," the girl continued as she appraised him from head to foot. "Not too fat, not too skinny." She leaned down to get a good look at his legs. "With calves like that, I'd say you're a football player. My brother has the same ones. No? Running track maybe? You look familiar, by the way. Should I know you from somewhere?"

Greg didn't know what to make of the girl. She was so… alive. And exuberant. Nothing like what he was used to at home. He didn't know how he was supposed to react.

The girl either didn't notice Greg's doubts or didn't care. "I'm Amélie, by the way," she prattled on. "I live just down the street. I usually come here for breakfast when I don't have to be at school until ten. I just love watching people walk by, wondering what they do for a living, who their friends are, where they're going. Don't you find that stuff fascinating?"

Greg continued staring, his mouth now hanging open.

She must have read something in his expression. "Oh, I'm not judging you for the whole sports thing, you know. It might not be obvious, with my cheeks taking up three quarters of my face and all, but I do lots of sports. I play volleyball, and I'm part of a circus group. I specialize in walking on a giant ball—it's just so much fun. Have you ever tried it?"

Greg managed a shake of his head.

A sandwich and the green glass of *diabolo menthe* appeared on the table in front of Greg. "That'll be seven euros, please," the waiter said.

Shaking himself back into the present, Greg pulled out a ten and waited for the waiter to give him his change.

The minute the man disappeared back inside the café, Amélie started talking again.

"Do you mind if I come join you?" she asked. "It'll keep you from getting a crick in your neck from turning like that."

Without waiting for Greg to reply, she left her seat, and brought her milkshake to Greg's table.

"I won't be able to people-watch as well from here," she said. "With my back to the square and all. But at least I can watch you. You seem interesting."

Greg had been ready to tell her to go back to her table, but her last comment changed his mind. She found him interesting? Nobody had ever told him that before. He'd always just been boring Greg, who never said anything in class or during football practice, and who was never allowed to go anywhere.

Deciding she probably wouldn't mind if he just stayed silent, he grabbed his sandwich and took a bite.

His eyes closed in bliss. He'd been hungrier that he'd realized. He'd had a decent meal last night, in some small village in the pass where roads and trains snaked into the basin occupied by Grenoble, but since then he'd walked through the night, allowing only two short stops for rest.

"You didn't get out of bed an hour ago," Amélie said.

Greg opened his eyes to meet hers but didn't stop chewing. He took another bite, figuring that would be a good excuse not to answer her statement.

"You look way too tired to have just gotten out of bed," Amélie insisted. The playful gleam in her eye from earlier was replaced by something more assessing. "I can smell you from here, you've been sweating in that t-shirt for *way* too long, and your legs can't seem to stop trembling."

Greg lowered his legs from the chair to the ground, but that didn't stop his muscles from spasming.

"Did you walk here?" Amélie's eyes were boring into Greg's now, her gaze amazingly intense for someone with such a cute and round face.

Greg took a sip of his drink. The coolness of the ice cubes and the sharp sting of the mint felt wonderful, but unfortunately, didn't help with changing the subject. Greg tried just keeping his mouth shut and finish his drink, but for some reason, Amélie didn't jump in to fill the silence.

When Greg reluctantly put his empty glass back on the table and took another bite of his sandwich, Amélie nodded as if to herself.

"You're here to pass over, aren't you?"

Greg's legs stilled under the table. His heart thumped a beat like his father practicing on his boxing ball, and his hands shook as they lowered to his lap, his sandwich finished.

"Don't worry," Amélie said, her voice soft and kind. "Nobody's judging you. But that's it, right?"

Greg gulped and nodded.

A moment of silence, then Amélie clapped her hands as if she were a teacher calling a class of ten-year-olds to order. "All right, then. I guess I'll have to help."

Greg straightened and his eyes shot to meet hers. "I don't need your help."

"Easy," Amélie said, her hands going up in surrender. "I didn't say you needed it. Eh...all right, I did say I *have to* help, didn't I. Yeah, that's not what I meant. I mean I'd love to help. I'm *good* at helping with this stuff."

"This stuff?"

"Passing over." Amélie's dark eyes suddenly seemed out of place in her face, as if she'd swapped them with an old lady's.

They stared at each other for what felt like an eternity. The waiter came to collect their empty glasses, the couple at the table next to them finished their coffees and left, and an old man settled in at their place to read his paper.

"Do you know what you want?" Amélie asked finally.

Greg's eyebrows drew together in a frown. "What I want?"

"Where do you want to pass over to?"

"There's…" Greg hated opening himself up to ridicule like this, but Amélie seemed like a really nice girl. He still had to force the words out. "There's more than one place I could go?"

"Place and place." Amélie tipped her head from one side to the other as she seemed to try on the taste of her words before letting them out of her mouth. "It's all the same place, really. You won't come out on the other side and find a beach resort or anything."

"But they say it's a different place."

"They do say that." Amélie's hand rubbed up and down her thigh. "But it's not the locale that's important. It's the people, the feelings, the actions. *Those* can be different."

Greg stared at her as his frustration rose in his chest. "I don't understand," he finally ground out through clenched teeth.

Amélie broke into a brilliant smile, her pensive expression dismissed in a second. "No worries! I'll explain it to you as we go."

"As we go?"

"Sure." She got up and grabbed Greg's hand, effectively dragging him out of his chair and after her across the square. Greg just barely managed to snatch his backpack along before it was left behind.

"They're all down in the city center," Amélie explained. "It's very rare for a bubble to appear at more than five hundred meters from the foot of the Bastille."

"A bubble?" Greg was so busy trying to keep up, both physically as she basically ran down the street, and mentally as she talked about things he'd never heard of before, that he wasn't even worried about looking stupid.

Amélie slowed down to allow Greg to catch up. "A bubble is what we call the portals that allow people to pass through to other worlds. They're in the shape of a sphere, and when they arrive, they always float down from the sky like God is up there having fun blowing bubbles."

They were back on the large avenue that Greg had walked down earlier, and it was even busier than before. Cars were crawling along at pedestrian speed in all four lanes, and the people walking to work or school advanced at a brisk pace, making Greg suspect that they were all running late for something or other.

Amélie weaved her way down the sidewalk, pulling Greg by the elbow, either because she was afraid he wouldn't be able to avoid a collision on his own, or to make sure he didn't make a run for it.

"Each bubble has its own…characteristics," Amélie explained. "You can make one type of request from it, not just anything." She met Greg's gaze. "Do you understand this? It's really important."

Greg shook his head.

She pulled on Greg's elbow again as she increased their speed. "There's this one bubble that's really popular, where you can get one person to change his views of you. Like, if your wife doesn't love you anymore, you can go to a world where she actually still does. Real popular with couples on the verge of divorce, obviously, but also with people who are convinced their parents don't love them."

She went silent as her gaze turned distant. "I've always wondered what happened with those people. I mean, logically, don't all parents love their kids? Maybe they just didn't know how to show it, or that they needed to show it better. So what happens when you ask the bubble to change how a person feels about you when that person is already feeling that thing?"

Greg had never felt more lost in a conversation, and had no answer to her question, but his mind was reeling with the possibilities.

Maybe he could go to a world where his parents loved him?

Except it seemed like you could only request the change in one person, so he'd have to choose between his mom and his dad. And he suspected that Amélie's theory was right; that his parents did love him, in their own way. It just wasn't a way that Greg could live with any longer.

"There's another one, right in the middle of Place Grenette," Amélie continued when it became clear that Greg had nothing to add to this conversation. "It's the biggest bubble I've ever seen—and I've made sure to see all the known ones—and it gives me the hives. You can ask for a person to not exist. Not for the person to die, but to never have existed."

Greg stopped in his tracks.

A world without his dad. How would his mom behave if his dad wasn't there to influence her, to make her want to change for him?

Amélie had walked on without Greg, but now she came storming back.

"Oh, no you don't!" she hissed in his face, an angry blush covering her cheeks. "You do *not* want to go there. Think about the consequences!" With a glance at the sky, she grabbed Greg's hand and pulled him with her at an even greater pace than before. "It's gonna be soon."

"What consequences?" Greg asked. He was really warming to the idea of a world without his father in it. Especially one where he'd never even existed. His mother wouldn't know to be sad, or to grieve him.

Amélie growled before answering. "Come on…" She stopped short, making Greg run right into her back. "What's your name again?"

"Greg," he said.

She nodded, then took off again. "Come on, Greg. You seem like a smart guy. Think about it."

Greg *was* thinking about it. It seemed absolutely brilliant. "What if you go through and ask to remove Hitler."

Amélie rolled her eyes. "Want to make a guess as to the number of people who have done just that?"

"Many?"

"Thousands."

She was slowing down, allowing Greg to catch up and walk next to her. They'd entered a large square, large enough to house the entire village he'd stopped in the night before.

In the center, in front of a wide staircase shaped like an amphitheater leading down to a Fnac store, stood a bubble the size of a small building.

It really was like the bubbles the girl next door had blown all through the summer between the fourth and the fifth grade. Transparent, but when the sunlight hit at a certain angle, colorful shapes moved across the surface, like rainbow colored eels playing hide and seek.

On the ground, a fence had been set up, keeping people away from the bubble. The only hole in the fence was a tiny cabin, with a line of four people in front of it. Behind them, two police officers stood guard, though they seemed bored.

"You've really never seen one before, huh?" Amélie said.

Greg realized they'd completely stopped, and he'd probably stood there staring like an idiot for several minutes.

"That's cool," she said lightly. "I mean, they only exist in Grenoble, so if you've never been…"

"So what does this one do?" he asked.

Amélie scowled at the bubble. "It's the one I was talking about. To erase a person's very existence."

Greg's feet moved forward, as if of their own accord.

"Greg!" Amélie caught up with him and grabbed his elbow. "You do not want to use that one. No matter what someone has done to you."

It's not just me, Greg thought as he dragged Amélie along with him toward the little cabin.

"Have you ever read that book by Stephen King?" Amélie asked. "The one where a guy goes back in time to stop the JFK murder?"

Greg shook his head.

"It's this really, really long book," she said. "For, like, five hundred pages, this guy's only goal is to get to the killer before he pulls the trigger. You read along, wondering if he's going to pull it off or not. Usually, the conclusion of stories like that is that you can't change the past."

Greg slowed for a second to glance at the girl hanging onto his elbow.

"What?" she said. "I'm interested in the subject. I've read a lot of books on time travel. Sue me. Anyway, in this book, he actually does manage to save JFK. And can you guess what happens?"

"I'd say the world is a better place," Greg said. He didn't really know much about American history, but he'd heard enough about that particular incident to know everybody considered it a catastrophe for humanity.

"See, that's not what happens in the book. JFK lives, but everything else goes to hell, and when the guy comes back to today, the world is about to go under. And it makes perfect sense."

Greg stopped to face Amélie. "So the world ends at the end of the book?"

Amélie glanced at the bubble, now only twenty meters away, before locking her gaze on Greg. "Well, Stephen King *is* the king of horror. But no. The guy goes back in time again to reset everything, lets JFK get killed, and calls it a day."

Greg frowned. "That's kind of anticlimactic."

"I'll lend you the book," Amélie said. "You'll see. And the point here is that the people who go through asking for Hitler to never have been born? I'm far from convinced they're going to a better place. Maybe Hitler coming to power meant that someone even worse wasn't able to. Maybe that other guy would have won the war, and we'd all be living under the rule of the Third Reich right now."

Greg frowned at her. It had sounded like such a good idea. But she was, unfortunately, making sense. Still, he didn't have to aim that high…

Amélie grabbed Greg's shoulders and shook him. "I can see what you're thinking, Greg. Stop it, right this minute. No matter who you're going for. Think about the consequences of removing just one person from the world. Like this one guy who was so frustrated by his father-in-law never warming to him. So he went through requesting the man never existed."

"What happened?" Greg asked.

"Well, I don't actually know, do I?" Amélie gave him a stern glare. "Nobody knows what happens once people go through. They never come back to tell us. But that one should be obvious. Tell me, Greg. If I remove the father from a family, how many kids do you think the mother will have, all on her own?"

Greg's breath caught. "It removes the kids?"

"Of course it does! The guy was never there to conceive the child!"

"So the guy went to a world where his father-in-law never existed, but then neither did his wife?"

"*Now* you're getting it. Seriously, that one is *so* dangerous. There's just no way to anticipate what might be changed by your request."

Greg stared longingly at the bubble towering above them. The oily colors swirled and shifted.

Damn her for making sense.

"Can I just go have a closer look?" he asked.

"Fine," Amélie conceded. "But I'm coming with you." She grabbed his hand and squeezed hard enough to make Greg wince.

As they reached the wooden cabin by the bubble, a man emerged from a door at its back. He was rather on the short side, had balding blond hair, and an angry scowl. He stepped right up to the bubble, then seemed to hesitate.

"Is he going through?" Greg asked. "How does it work?"

"All you need is for your skin to touch the bubble," Amélie said. "Then on this side you go poof, and you'll appear in the other world."

"But nobody ever comes back?"

She shook her head.

"Then how do we know how it works? How can we be sure the people don't just cease to exist? Or even if they work, that they work the way you say they do."

Amélie's gaze was on the man in front of the bubble, but Greg didn't think she was actually seeing him. "I just know. I can feel it."

The man reached out toward the roiling surface of the bubble. His hand touched the surface.

He disappeared.

No popping sound, no flash, no nothing.

"That's also kind of anticlimactic," Greg said.

The three persons still waiting in line exchanged excited glances. They were clearly waiting for it to be their turn. The police officers scanned the crowd, making Greg think this might be the moment when someone could possibly try to do something dangerous or illegal.

Greg locked eyes with one of the officers for a second, before the man turned to say something to his colleague.

"He won't be any better off on the other side," Amélie said, still that distant look on her face, as if she was listening to something only she could hear.

It didn't feel like she was theorizing. "How do you know?" Greg asked.

"I can feel it," she explained. "Some of us just can." Her eyes scanned the circumference of the bubble and she sighed. "I can feel what you can wish for, and I can feel a remnant of what the people who go through feel about the world they've arrived in.

"Some bubbles give mostly positive results. For example, there's this one tiny red bubble that allows you to undo one action you regret. If you don't go too far back in time and choose something that will have minimum impact—for example, just on you and one other person—you can come out a winner."

Her eyes still on the bubble, Amélie suddenly winced. She started moving away, pulling Greg along by the hand. "Come on, let's go."

"What happened?"

"He realized he'd have been better off not going through," Amélie said. "Like ninety-nine percent of the people who use this one."

As they passed the cabin, Greg caught a glimpse of a poster on one of its walls.

"Two thousand euros! That's insane!"

"That's the cost of entering a parallel universe," Amélie said. She was pulling Greg along toward a narrow street winding away from the far corner of the square.

"It should be expensive, by the way," she added. "Or everyone would go through on a whim and we'd have nobody left on this side."

Greg would have no choice but to stay on this side if that was how much it cost to pass through. He now had less than eighty euros, and no way to get any more.

His feelings must have shown on his face because Amélie stopped just as they entered the narrow street and gave him a hug. "Don't worry, Greg. We'll figure something out. Maybe we could make things better for you in *this* world?"

Tears threatened, but Greg fought them back. He was not going to cry in front of this girl. And he was not going to cry out of self-pity; that was in the past. The present Greg had a plan, and he was going to go through with it.

He was about to tell Amélie as much when she suddenly jerked and her head snapped up, her gaze going to the sky.

"There's a new one," she whispered.

"A new what?"

"A new bubble. It's been brewing for days. Even the people who usually can't feel a thing have known this one was coming." She took off down the street—la Grande Rue according to a plate on the wall—once again pulling Greg along for the ride.

"Come on," she said. "I need to know what it does."

Greg hurried to keep up. "I thought you didn't like people using them."

"Which is why I need to know what it does. Whenever a new bubble appears, there's always some idiot who goes through completely blind, not caring what it does, just that it's free until the city can set up a perimeter."

After a turn and another narrow cobbled street lined with tall stone buildings, Amélie brought them to a stop in a public park. On their left stood a preschool with a tiny courtyard, and on their right, just across the river, the Bastille rose into the mist.

"They always appear near the Bastille," Amélie said. She seemed to be scanning the rose bushes in the park as she talked. "We've not understood the significance of the mountain yet, but it plays some sort of role, that's for sure."

She went down on all fours and crawled along the path next to a bush of yellow roses. "Why is it so hard to find?" she muttered to herself. "My entire body is humming with the power. I can't believe it's a small one. Ah—here it is."

She whisked a pair of rubber gloves out of the front pocket of her jeans and snapped them on. Very carefully, she inserted a hand into the rose bush. It came back with a bright pink bubble the size of a ping pong ball.

"Should you be touching that?" After all her speeches, Greg couldn't understand why she would risk passing through on accident.

"It needs to be in contact with your skin for it to take you away," Amélie explained. "Any kid could find it in there. It's not safe to let them lie just anywhere."

"Then why haven't they moved the one we saw earlier?"

Amélie sat down on a bench on the other side of the path and brought the ball up to eye level.

"Because it's too big to move without risk," she said. "And it's been secured. And it's a major tourist attraction. So the city is just fine with it staying put."

"They all belong to the city?" Greg sat down on the bench next to Amélie and dropped his backpack to the ground. His t-shirt was still as disgustingly soaked as earlier, but at least his lungs seemed to have adapted somewhat to the climate.

"Yes," Amélie replied. "At first it was a first arrived, first served kind of thing, but that got out of hand real quick, and a law was passed to give ownership to the city where the bubble first appeared."

"I thought this only happened in Grenoble."

Amélie winked. "It does. But in case it starts somewhere else, the law is ready for it."

"Should you be moving it around? Won't the city mind?"

Amélie was rolling the ball from the palm of one hand to the other. Though it was pink and opaque, it wasn't just one color. Like with the larger bubble earlier, there were shapes shifting around on the surface, except they were hundreds of different hues of pink. It was mesmerizing.

"It's fine," she said absently. "I've done this before."

She had a portal to a different world in the palm of her hand. If Greg reached out and touched it, he would be transported somewhere else. Somewhere very similar to this world, but with one thing different.

"So what does it do?" he asked. Greg was starting to understand the need for the city to protect the new bubbles. The temptation to just reach out and get the pass for free was overwhelming. Who cared what it did. He just needed to wish for something to change with his dad, and the other side was bound to be an improvement.

"Working on it." Amélie kept rolling the ball between her hands, sometimes blowing on it, sometimes holding it close to her ear to listen.

"In a way it seems very similar to the big one on Place Grenette." The frown on Amélie's forehead showed how little she liked that idea. "But it's also the complete opposite."

"Okay…"

Amélie brought the bubble up right in front of her nose. Her eyes crossed a little as she stared at the moving lines.

"The action is on the existence of the person you place your wish on." She shook her head. "But I don't feel the destruction that oozes out of the other one."

Greg had trouble following. He could reach out, wish for his father to disappear, and he'd be golden.

A hand clamped down on his. "Don't you dare!" Amélie hissed. "Not before we know what it does. Actually, probably not even then. These things are not benign."

"Maybe some of them are," Greg argued. "You just haven't run into any of the constructive ones yet."

Amélie drew in a sharp breath. "That's it. It creates instead of destroys."

"Huh?"

Amélie's eyes went wide and she regarded the pink bubble with an awe Greg wouldn't have thought her capable of.

"You wish for someone to exist, and you end up in a world where they do."

"Like bringing someone back to life?"

"No," she whispered. "Like wishing for your soul mate to exist, and then he does."

Movement caught Greg's attention. Two police officers—seemed like the two who'd been guarding the bubble earlier—were approaching down the path.

"Grégoire Lefebvre?" one of them asked.

Greg froze.

"Oh, shit," Amélie whispered. The hand holding the bubble lowered to her lap and she seemed to be looking at Greg a lot more closely than she had up until then. "You're that kid who disappeared in Lyon three days ago. I knew your face rang a bell."

The officers stood in front of the bench, effectively closing off all escape routes. "Your parents have been worried sick looking for you, young man," the first officer said.

"My…parents?" Greg's voice cracked on the last word.

"Yes, your parents. They should be here shortly. They weren't too far away since they spent the night in the village you apparently went through yesterday."

"Grégoire!" His dad's voice must have been heard by half the city. He came striding across the park, his huge arms swinging and his brows drawn together in a dangerous line.

Greg tried to make a run for it, but the officers anticipated him.

"Running will only make it worse," the one holding him in place said under his breath.

"Well," Greg's dad said in a tone that promised a lot of unpleasant things once they got home, "I wish I could say I was surprised. I'm not. You keep doing your best to be a disappointment to your mother and I, and I think it's the *one* thing we can count on you to excel at."

Amélie's eyes jumped between Greg and his dad, understanding dawning. Luckily, she didn't say anything.

That would only have made things worse.

She did, however, get up to stand next to Greg. She still held the bubble, but she'd curled her fingers around it protectively. Greg didn't think his father or the police officers realized what she was holding.

Greg's dad stalked up to stand in front of Greg, towering over him.

"I wish I'd had a different son," he said.

Greg saw a flash of pink and heard Amélie gasp. The bubble crashed into his dad's face and popped on impact.

"I'm so sorry!" Amélie yelled. "I didn't think!" She brought her hands up to her mouth, but when Greg's dad didn't disappear, she slowly lowered them.

"Come on, Dad," a male voice said from behind Greg. "Calm down, will you? He just needed a break. I knew where he was the whole time."

Greg turned, as if in slow motion, to face…his brother.

He'd never had a brother. He was an only child.

Except…he wasn't.

The information tore through his brain like a tidal wave. For a while, he could remember both hiding alone in the garden shed when his dad was angry and looking for him and hanging out in his brother's room because his big brother was taking care of him while his dad was busy with work.

It worked its way through his entire life and left behind a completely different boy with completely different memories. He still had the ghost of a memory of what had just happened.

"It's completely reversed," Amélie whispered to herself. "Everything is backwards. Oh God, this changes everything."

She grabbed Greg's face with both hands and stared into his eyes. "Greg, how do you feel?"

"Great," Greg replied. "I feel great." He really did.

Like he always did when he hung out with his brother.

THANK YOU

THANK YOU FOR reading *Unexpected Consequences*. I hope you enjoyed it! I certainly had fun going for a quick (imaginary) trip back to Grenoble, where I spent a year in my youth.

If you liked the story, you might want to check out some of my other books mentioned on the next page. It's mostly Mysteries, but a few other genre short stories will pop up, too.

And don't forget that the first book of my *Tolosa Mystery* series, *The Red Brick Haze*, is available for free on my website.

R.W. Wallace
www.rwwallace.com

Also by R.W. Wallace

Mystery

The Tolosa Mystery Series
The Red Brick Haze (free)
The Red Brick Cellars
The Red Brick Basilica

Ghost Detective Shorts (coming soon)
Just Desserts
Lost Friends
Family Bonds
Till Death
Family History
Common Ground
Heritage
Eternal Bond
New Beginnings

Short Stories
Cold Blue Eternity
Hidden Horrors
Critters
Gertrude and the Trojan Horse
First Impressions
Let Them Eat Cake
Out of Sight
Two's Company
Like Mother Like Daughter

Fantasy (short stories)
Unexpected Consequences
Morbier Impossible
A Second Chance

Science Fiction (short stories)
The Vanguard

Lollapalooza Shorts
Quarantine
Common Enemies
Coiled Danger
Mars Meeting

Adventure (short stories)
Size Matters

ABOUT THE AUTHOR

R.W. WALLACE WRITES in most genres, though she tends to end up in mystery more often than not. Dead bodies keep popping up all over the place whenever she sits down in front of her keyboard.

The stories mostly take place in Norway or France; the country she was born in and the one that has been her home for two decades. Don't ask her why she writes in English—she won't have a sensible answer for you.

Her Ghost Detective short story series appears in *Pulphouse Magazine*, starting in issue #9.

You can find all her books, long and short, all genres, on rwwallace.com.

www.ingramcontent.com/pod-product-compliance
Lightning Source LLC
LaVergne TN
LVHW041717060526
838201LV00043B/781